For Lois Leon

ISBN 0-590-63519-0

Copyright © 1998 by Nord-Süd Verlag AG, Gossau Zürich, Switzerland.
First published in Switzerland under the title *Wie Leo wieder König wurde*.
English translation copyright © 1998 by North-South Books Inc. All rights reserved.
Published by Scholastic Inc., 555 Broadway, New York, NY 10012,
by arrangement with North-South Books Inc.
SCHOLASTIC and associated logos are trademarks and/or
registered trademarks of Scholastic Inc.

12 11 10 9 8 7 6 5 4 3 2 1   8 9/9 0 1 2 3/0

Printed in the U.S.A.   14

First Scholastic printing, September 1998

MARCUS PFISTER

How Leo Learned to Be King

Translated by J. Alison James

SCHOLASTIC INC.
New York Toronto London Auckland Sydney

Leo the lion, King of the Beasts, woke one day from
a nice long nap. He stretched and scratched his back on
his throne. He yawned loudly. Then he opened his jaws
wide and let out a bloodcurdling roar that shook the entire
savannah.

"Be quiet!" snapped a little warthog who happened to
be trotting by. "Your ceaseless roaring is getting on my
nerves. You're driving all the animals crazy!"

Leo couldn't believe his ears. He stared open-mouthed at the warthog. Nobody had ever dared to speak to him that way!

"Just who do you think you're talking to? I am Leo, the Invincible, the King of the Beasts!" And with that, Leo tensed to spring at the warthog and strike him down with one powerful paw.

Luckily, a water buffalo happened to hear the argument and rushed in between them.

"Whoa—hold on a minute," the buffalo said to Leo. "We don't need a King of the Beasts anymore. We can take care of ourselves."

"Yeah," piped up the warthog, peeking out from behind the buffalo. "Like he said, we animals can make it on our own."

Leo gasped. He clutched at his heart and moaned. "Oh, whatever have I done to deserve this? I was always—"

"You were always a lazy show-off!" squawked the
vulture as he swooped down and snatched Leo's crown.
"What have *you* ever done to deserve to be our king?"
 More and more animals gathered, circling around Leo.
The rhinoceros, the elephant, the hyena, the zebra, even the
gentle giraffe all talked at once, shouting wildly and trying
to make themselves heard in the din. But then they joined
together to shout in chorus:

> *Lazy Leo, you must step down.*
> *Get off the throne. Give up your crown!*

There was nothing Leo could do except flee from the rebellious animals. He escaped into the tall grass near a stand of trees. "We'll just see how they get along without me," he thought defiantly.

But after a while he had to admit to himself that he had never done much of anything for the animals. What he really liked to do was lie around lazily, being waited on and admired. "I deserve to be served because I am the King of the Beasts!" he thought. "It has always been this way. Why should I change?"

Day after day Leo prowled around the savannah, wondering how the animals were managing without him.

They were managing quite well, in fact. Nobody seemed to notice he was gone, and the animals went about their lives as usual.

One afternoon Leo heard a whimpering sound from the side of the river. He peered through the grass, and there, crouched on the riverbank, was a small mouse.

"Why are you crying?" growled Leo.

The mouse took one look at the huge lion and began to shake and stutter: "Uh-uh-uh, Leo! I j-j-just wanted to get to the other s-s-side of this big river. B-b-but I c-c-can't make it."

"This little brook?" said Leo. "Nothing to it. Just climb on my back and hold tight to my mane."

Then the lion crouched and took a flying leap across the water.

"Oh, my!" said the mouse, slipping down from Leo's back. "Oh, my, that was amazing. Thank you very much."

"It was my pleasure," said Leo. "Take care, little mouse."

A few days later the lion was walking along when suddenly he felt the earth begin to shake. Leo barely had time to duck behind a bush before a charging rhinoceros thundered by!

"A full-grown lion is no match for a raging rhino," thought Leo. He sneezed and shook the dust from his mane.

From beyond the bushes he heard a voice: "Hey, rhino! What are you doing?" Surprised, Leo pushed apart the branches of his hiding place.

It was a porcupine, hopping around, his quills twitching in fury.

"Hey," called the lion. "What's wrong?"

"That bellowing beast trampled my beautiful burrow."

"Take it easy," said Leo, coming out from the bushes. "I'll help you mend your home."

Once his burrow was repaired, the porcupine was much more cheerful. "Thank you," he said to the lion.

"You're very welcome," said Leo. "But now I'm worried about the rhinoceros. I wonder what was bothering him."

It took quite a while for Leo to find the rhinoceros. He was lying under a tree, stunned and moaning. Right above his two horns a third had sprung up: a huge pink bump.

"What happened to you?" asked Leo, shocked.

The rhino groaned. "First I was stung by a wasp. It hurt so much that I ran and ran, and I didn't watch where I was going and crashed right into this tree!"

Leo found some moist leaves and used them to cool the bump and take away the sting.

"You'd better stay here and rest," he said. "I'll come back later to make sure you're all right."

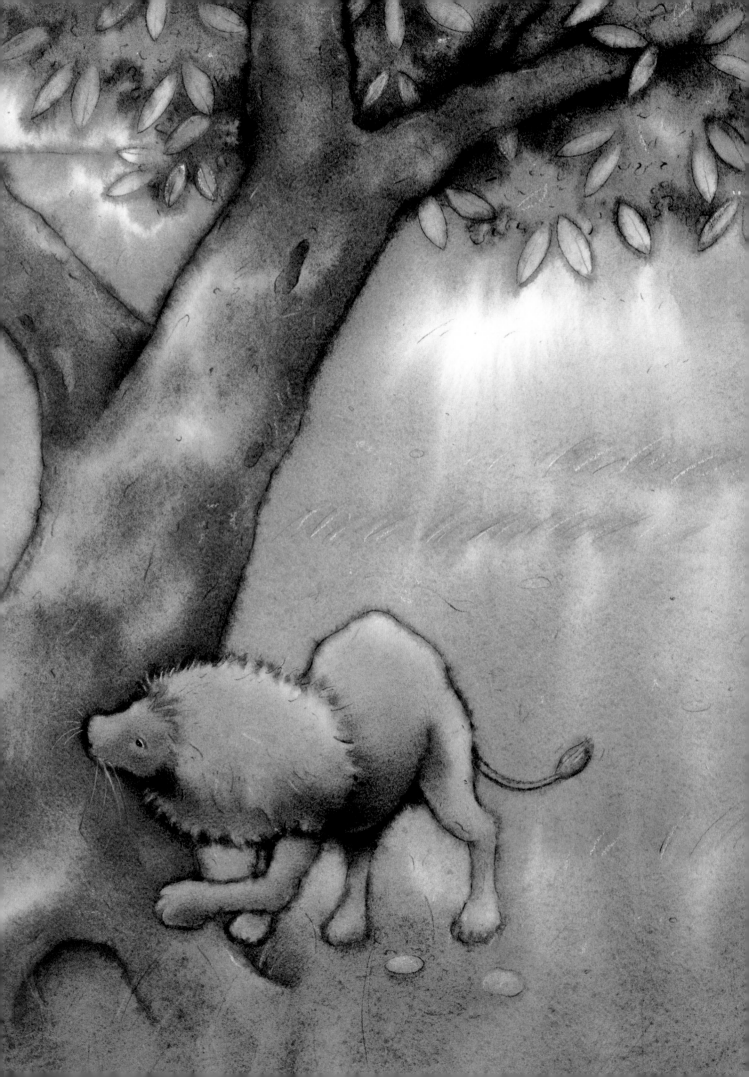

That evening, when the animals met at the watering hole as usual, they were telling stories of how helpful the lion had been. Everyone was astonished to hear what had happened.

"That's the kind of king I'd like to have," trumpeted the elephant. "Someone who cares about you."

"Yes!" yelped the hyena. "Someone who's kind. Someone who notices the smallest things."

"That's our kind of king!" they all declared.

The very next day, the animals went to find Leo. They brought him his crown and throne.

The water buffalo cleared his throat and spoke in a gruff voice. "Um, Leo, we decided we want you back. Will you be our king again?"

Leo was surprised and very touched. "My dear friends," he said. "I am delighted that you want me back. It would be a privilege to serve you." He looked around. "But I don't need a crown and a throne to rule. After all, while I may be king, I'm still just an animal like all of you."